CRICKET

CRICKET

Dorothy Hamilton

Illustrated by Paul Van Demark

HERALD PRESS
Scottdale, Pennsylvania
Kitchener, Ontario
1975

Library of Congress Cataloging in Publication Data

Hamilton, Dorothy, 1906-
  Cricket.

  SUMMARY: Ten-year-old Dale's dreams seem to come
true when his family moves to a farm in the country and
gets a pony.
  [1. Family life -- Fiction. 2. Ponies -- Fiction]
I. Van Demark, Paul, ill. II. Title.
PZ7.H18136Cr   [Fic]   74-30421
ISBN 0-8361-1760-3
ISBN 0-8361-1761-1 pbk.

CRICKET
Copyright © 1975 by Herald Press, Scottdale, Pa. 15683
Library of Congress Card Catalog Number: 74-30421
International Standard Book Number:
    0-8361-1760-3   (hardcover)
    0-8361-1761-1   (softcover)
Printed in the United States of America
Design by Alice B. Shetler

To Dale

1

Dale Martin had dreamed of having a pony for almost as long as he could remember. There were pictures in his mind which were almost real. He saw himself riding a light brown pony with a silky mane and three white feet. Sometimes he rocked as the pony trotted. Sometimes he leaned forward on the animal's neck with his hair blowing as they raced against the wind. And in some of his wide-awake dreams he slowed the pony to a walk so he could hear the clip-clop of its feet.

Dale had only been on horseback five or six times in his life. He had ridden a few times when they stopped to see his mother's cousin on the way to California. This was way out in Sioux City, Iowa. And he'd paid twenty cents to ride a tired Shetland three times around a roped-in circle at the county fair.

It was Dale's father who helped make the idea of owning a pony seem wonderful and exciting. "I never had any pets of my own," Fred Martin often said. "But I did visit a cousin on a farm for a week every summer."

"Did you ride a lot?" Dale always asked. He knew the answer. This was the way conversations about owning a pony started. And they always ended with Mr. Martin drawing a big breath and saying, "Believe me, boy, just as soon as I can manage to get hold of a small farm, the next step will be to go looking for a pony. You keep on saving your money."

Dale had begun to think that time would never come. He hadn't told anyone yet that he felt this way. "Maybe I don't want it to be true," he thought. But on a spring

8

evening the thoughts slipped out into words. "Dad, will we ever find a place?"

They were sitting on the bench that went all the way around the big oak tree in the backyard. No one else was near. They never talked about the pony when his mother was around. Dale didn't know why. The whole family except the baby said a lot about moving to the country. Mrs. Martin wanted room to raise canna bulbs to sell. And Dale's sister wanted lots of room to ride her two-wheeler.

"Getting discouraged, are you?" Mr. Martin asked.

"Well, maybe," Dale said. "Tired of waiting, anyway."

"I suppose that's natural," his father said. "Time doesn't seem to move at the same pace for you as it does for me."

"I get to thinking I'll be too old for a pony some of these days. But I'd still want a riding horse, one that was bigger."

"Don't give up on me," Mr. Martin said. "A medium-sized animal would do this family more good. Either Katie or

Jane may take a liking for riding, too. I'll just have to look harder -- maybe change my ideas about what would suit me."

"What do you mean -- change your ideas?"

"Well, I've sort of been set on moving to the north, in between here and the city. That would shorten the trips when I have to go to the wholesale house. Could be I've put blinders on when I looked in the other directions."

Dale looked sideways at his father. "Is he saying he's been wrong?" he thought. Grown-ups don't do that very often. They usually sound like they know everything and don't make mistakes."

He felt a little more hopeful that evening. Surely they'd have a better chance of finding a place if they really looked in four directions instead of one. Before he went to sleep he wondered if it would be warm enough that his mother would let him go swimming at Meadow Lark Pool. Spring had been slow in coming. Or had

10

winter been poky about leaving?

The smell of frying bacon came up the stairs the next morning and tempted him to jump out of bed. The baby was in the high chair banging her short-handled spoon against the metal tray. "Don't they ever make those things padded?" Dale's father asked.

"I'd hope not," Frances Martin said. "They'd be quite a laundry problem. She will quit when I cut her egg and toast for her."

Dale didn't even get a chance to ask about going swimming. His father took charge of his day by saying, "I could use some help this morning. We got a shipment of paint last night."

"Isn't it too late in the season to be restocking paint?" Mrs. Martin asked, as she tied a fuzzy bib around the baby's neck.

"It's never too late when you're out of some colors. I guess the late spring kept a lot of folks from getting in the mood to fix up. We've had a rush the last two days."

No one asked Dale if he wanted to help.

He didn't expect them to do so. The Martins worked together and they did fun things together sometimes.

"You'd better change your T-shirt," Dale's mother said. "That one's all stretched out of shape at the neck."

Ten minutes later Dale and his father left the house by the back door and crossed the alley which was covered with crushed stone. Some rocks were sharp. Dale could feel them through the soles of his sneakers. They cut across to Fulton Street and stopped in front of the real estate office.

Dale could never remember a single time when his father hadn't stopped to read the "New Listings." Even if it was raining, or the red line of the thermometer hadn't crept above zero, he'd glance at the board which posted places for sale.

Dale had quit looking. Everyone seemed to want to buy what they were hunting, small acreages with good buildings. About the only places ever for sale were big farms, or places in Parker City or Muncie.

He walked ahead of his father and looked in the drugstore window. There wasn't much that was new. Just girls' stuff, perfume and hair clasps and fat pink or blue curlers. He shaded his eyes with one hand trying to see if there were any new model cars on the wire rack.

"Hey, Dale," his father called. "Come here! Look!"

"Dad's excited," Dale thought. "I can tell. He always rubs the side of his head with a fist when he's real keen about something."

"I'm going in and see Kirk," Fred Martin said. "Even if customers have to wait for me to open the store."

"Why?" Dale asked. "Is there a place for sale?"

"Sure is," his father said. "Twenty acres. Out south, beyond Crystal Pool Bridge."

In the ten minutes before Dale and his dad opened the hardware store several things happened. Kirk, the real estate agent, said he'd call the owner and set up a time for the Martins to see the place. And Dale was told to call his mother and ask if she could go look at it during the noon hour.

"Who'll run the store?" she asked. "I thought this was such a busy time."

When Dale relayed the question his father said, "I'll get someone. Tell her that a couple of my loafers have parked themselves on the benches long enough to pick up a lot of know-how."

Dale worked hard for over two hours putting cans of paint on the shelves. He was surprised when his father said he'd done a good job. He'd tried to keep all the green shades together and not mix up yellows with reds. But it wasn't easy. For one thing the paint companies kept changing names. Greens were called Avocado, Heather, Jungle Moss, or Cypress. And he couldn't decide whether Coral, Sand, and Seashell should be stacked with the pinks or browns.

There was a rush of business around eleven o'clock and Dale began to wonder if his father would leave the store in the hands of Mr. Stone and Uncle Deke. These were the two old friends who sat around the store more than anyone else. Dale once heard his dad say they were probably the loneliest souls in town, that they had no relatives left.

"Even Uncle Deke?" Dale had asked. "Isn't he uncle to anyone?"

"He never was," his father said. "He wandered in here thirty or forty years ago. Was a section hand on the railroad. Liked the place and stayed when the work train pulled out. How he got tagged uncle I never heard."

Dale always liked to hear Deke Simpson talk. He had a lot of tales about faraway places. Some he told the same way every time and some he changed with every telling. It was easy to listen to him if you didn't try to figure out what was true and what wasn't.

Today no one listened to Uncle Deke except Mr. Stone, and he dozed now and then. Dale didn't stop even on his favorite story of the wreck of the circus train. He was too far away from the benches to hear above the banging of the paint cans and he didn't have time to listen.

The store was clear of customers by eleven-forty so Dale and his father left. "We'll be back in an hour," he told the bench-sitters. "Not many come in around noon. Either sell at what you think is right, make a note of what they take, or tell them to come back later."

Within twenty minutes the Martins were pulling in the wide gate at the end of a short graveled lane.

"Oh, look at all the trees and the lane," Dale said as they got out of the car. "Places to swing and ride my bike."

"And the house," Frances Martin said. "It looks like my grandmother's. It had a wide veranda. And lots of trees. I can't wait until I see the inside."

"Then don't," Fred Martin said. "Here's the key. We'll explore the barn. Right, Dale?"

"Right."

16

"Look at all the trees and the lane," Dale said. "Places to swing and ride my bike."

2

The minute Dale stepped into the shadowy barn he began to feel he'd already moved. His feet stirred up dust from the sifting of hay that covered the narrow feeding room floor. It rose and danced in the golden sunbeams that slanted through the four-pane window in the horse stall.

Dale hung over the manger from which animals once had eaten and looked at the square, boxed-off section. He didn't have to try to picture a pony. In his mind it was already there. He'd seen it dozens, maybe hundreds of times.

The pony of Dale's dreams was always

brown, like the stain from walnut shells. He didn't know why this was so. He could have pictured a dapple-gray or spotted pinto or an animal with the caramel color of a palomino.

His father lifted the baby from the stroller. They walked to the end of the passageway and opened the door to the granary. Dale leaned over and scraped a handful of scratchy oats from the bin. "Here's some feed," he said. "Could we use this?"

"Well, I don't know," his father answered. "Hard to tell how long it's been there. It could be moldy."

Dale climbed the slatted ladder that led to the haymow. "You can look," his father said. "But don't walk around. A lot of times boards crack and splinter under the weight of loads of hay. I'd want this checked before you kids played up there."

"Do you think we can buy it, Dad?"

"Well, I tell you, son. I'm going to try mighty hard. At first glance this is nearer to what we all want, except little Skeezicks here, than anything we've seen."

"She'd probably like it," Dale said. "Janie, I mean. When she's old enough to know one place from the other."

"We'd better get back to the house. Your mama will want us to look around."

Dale's sister, Katie, met them in the long sun-filled room that had to be the kitchen. Cabinets ran across one end and a metal sink unit sat in a nearby corner.

"It's a delish house, Daddy," Katie said. "The upstairs rooms have windows which stick out over the roof."

"Dormers," her father said. "I noticed as we drove in."

"I always did want to live in a place where there was a window seat. But there is none -- just the place for one."

"That'd be no problem," her father answered. "Some planks and padding and a little elbow grease is all it'd take."

"Elbow grease?" Katie said.

"He means work, silly," Dale explained.

"I'd like to know why you think you know everything," Katie said. "After all you're only two years older than I am."

"Well I knew that," Dale said. "You didn't hear Dad say I was wrong, did you?"

Katie didn't answer. She was halfway up the narrow stairs and was calling, "Slowpoke. Slowpoke!"

"That's the way she is," Dale thought. "If you don't let her get ahead of you one way she tries another."

"Where's your mother?" Fred Martin asked as he came to the foot of the stairway.

"She's up here," Katie said. "In the attic. Looking for treasures."

"And I found some too," Dale's mother said in a muffled voice. Dale traced the sound to a wooden door in a sloping wall of a side room. He couldn't see anything at first. When his eyes got adjusted to the dim light he could see his mother at the end of the attic. "What kind of treasures?" he asked.

"Picture frames," she answered. "Thick with scrollwork, leaf designs, and something that feels like tiny birds. I can't see too plainly."

Dale didn't think old picture frames were much of a treasure but if they were to his mother he wouldn't spoil her fun. She didn't ever say he was silly about what he collected. Not the butterflies, or Indian head pennies, or his new rock collection. He already had two chunks of tiger's-eye, a sample of pink quartz, and two pieces of Apache tears. He was saving money now to buy a piece of amethyst from the Gem Shop in Muncie. Some day he hoped to own a real star sapphire. That day might be a long time coming. Some things were. Like the day when he'd have a pony.

"Well," Frances Martin said as she stooped to come through the attic door. "Did the barn pass your inspection?"

"It sure did," Dale said. "It has room for a pony and a lot left over. And the barn would be a great place to play."

Dale's father walked to the head of the stairs. "If you've given this place the once-over," he said, "we'd better head back to town. We'll have to get a bite to eat."

"Didn't I tell you?" Mrs. Martin said. "I brought sandwiches and fruit. You saw the brown paper bag."

"I thought it was extra gear for the baby," Mr. Martin said.

"I didn't bring anything to drink. Do you suppose the water's good here?"

"I'm sure it is. The owner just moved out, remember."

The Martins went to the backyard and sat in the grass under a tall tree. Its spreading branches didn't keep all the silvery sunshine from them. The leaves were only tiny buds.

"That's an apple tree," Dale's father said.

"Delish," Katie said. "It'll be great to have a real for sure apple tree in our very own yard."

"Now, honey, don't get too excited," her mother said. "We haven't bought this place yet. And maybe we can't. It could be more than we can afford. And we don't know about the furnace or --" She didn't finish the sentence. Janie had crawled off the folded blanket and was chewing a fallen twig.

Dale looked at his father. "Is he thinking we can't buy this place? Mom always has a bunch of doubts about stuff," Dale thought. "Dad doesn't look worried. His eyes are bright -- sort of excited." That look always made Dale feel good.

His father and mother talked all the way back to town. He tried to hear everything they said but that wasn't easy. Katie was either chattering or trying to get the baby to talk. So he leaned forward and rested his arms on the back of the front seat.

"I don't think we should rush into this," Frances Martin said.

"Don't you like the house?"

"Oh yes. It has great possibilities," Dale's mother said. "And that special quality which can only be called hominess. And I could see acres and acres of blooming cannas. Yellow, pink, white, and red

24

-- even a few lavender. Although those bulbs are terribly expensive."

"Then why the cautious attitude?"

"Oh, I don't know. It's my nature, I guess," Dale's mother said. "I'm so afraid we'll make a mistake. Lose what we have -- as my father did about six times."

"Well I can see why you feel as you do," Mr. Martin said. "But I have the feeling this place won't stay on the market long. Someone will grab it. I'd like to be the one."

"Then go ahead. See what you can do," she said. "Just because I'm scared to take two steps ahead doesn't mean I should hold you back."

Dale sat back on the seat. He felt a little more hopeful. He wondered what his dad would do next and how soon.

He watched the fence posts as they passed them. "Only it looks like they are going past us," he thought. He saw a train moving along like a square-sided snake. Then he remembered. "I talked about the pony to Mom. She didn't say anything.

25

Does that mean she wouldn't care if I had one? Or didn't she really listen? Sometimes grown-ups don't. They nod or even answer. But you can tell they don't know what you say. Not all of it anyway."

3

Dale stayed close to his father during the rest of spring vacation. He wanted to know what was going on. When Fred Martin went to Winchester to see the banker about getting a loan, Dale asked if he could go along.

"Wouldn't you rather go over to Rick's?" his father asked. "I can hear basketballs thumping against the bank boards from here."

"Well, that'd be okay," Dale said. "But I'd rather know what you find out."

"I may not get a final decision today," his father said. "They may have to bring

27

the application up before a board."

Dale drew a deep breath which was really a sigh. Grown-ups were slow about a lot of important things. It seemed like they wasted so much time talking back and forth about what to do. They couldn't seem to see the good parts and go ahead. They seemed scared of what might be bad.

Dale remembered how it was when he wanted a bike. He'd saved more than half the money needed. And his parents never said they didn't want to pay for a bike. But they spent a lot of time talking. Was he old enough? Traffic through town was a lot heavier since the new school was built out south. His mother asked his father how old he was when he first had a two-wheeler. She tried to remember when her cousin Mark was considered old enough to ride. They wasted a whole week -- or was it nine days -- trying to decide. Dale kept thinking he could have done a lot of riding in that time.

Waiting now was even harder. The decision was more important. Sometimes Dale thought he couldn't bear it if they didn't get to move. "Already this place doesn't seem like home. Would it ever if we have to stay?" he wondered.

He didn't have to wait nine days for the answers to his questions. A telephone call settled the matter. It came early on Saturday morning. Dale was awake but not out of bed. It was raining, but not hard. He could hear drops hitting the window in little clicks. The white curtains danced inward in the morning breeze. It carried the sweet smell of the lilac blossoms from the bush in the side yard.

"If it rains all morning what can I do?" Dale thought. He hunched his shoulders deeper into the feather pillows. "If we lived on the farm I could play in the barn. And if I had my pony I could brush and curry its coat." He knew about currycombs. His dad sold them in the hardware store. Even if farmers did use tractors for power, a lot of people had horses for pleasure. The veterinarian out toward Mooreland raised ponies for sale and someone over west of Muncie had a lot of Arabians.

Dale was drifting off into sleep again when the telephone rang. He heard heavy footsteps come from the direction of the kitchen. "Dad's still home," he thought.

When his father said, "Yes, Mr. Thorne --" Dale sat up in bed so quickly his pillow fell to the floor. Mr. Thorne was the banker.

Dale tiptoed to the hall and leaned over the stair railing. He could see the top of his father's head and hear every word he said. "Yes. . . . They did? . . . . I see. . . . That should do it. . . . We can manage the balance. . . . I appreciate this call. . . . Yes. We'll be there. . . . Monday at nine."

By this time Dale was downstairs and his mother was in from the kitchen. Fred Martin reached over and rubbed the top of Dale's head as he smiled and said, "Well, it looks like we'll be moving. The last stumbling block's out of the way. The loan was approved."

At first Dale couldn't believe that this dream was coming true. He shook his head to be sure he was awake. He followed his parents to the kitchen, but this time he was the one who didn't listen carefully. He heard his mother ask, "Would it be better to sell or rent this place?" But he didn't pay any attention to the answer. This wasn't important to him.

Instead he began to wonder how long it would be until they moved. "And the next thing. When will we go looking for a pony?"

He wanted to break into the conversation and ask. But something told him this wasn't the time. Grown-ups couldn't seem to handle two questions at a time. Maybe that was because they spent so much time talking about every single one.

"Besides," Dale thought as he reached for a second cheese muffin, "it'd be better to talk to Dad alone. I know he thinks I'm old enough for a pony. Mom might think it'd be dangerous. Or that we can't afford both a farm and a pony. Or that feed would cost too much. She knows a lot of ways to worry."

"What's the next move?" Frances Martin asked as she refilled Dale's glass with orange juice.

"Well," Dale's father answered, "I'll stop by the real estate office. Tell them we got the loan. From then on **we** make the decisions and do the planning."

"My goodness," Frances said. "There certainly will be a lot of decisions. The first thing I want to do is go out to the farm and measure windows and floors. I wonder how many of our curtains and rugs we can use."

"Why not tomorrow?" Dale's father said. "If the weather clears we could take a picnic lunch and go out after church."

"That'd be great," Dale said. "I could do a lot of exploring. Hey, Dad. I can tell the kids we're moving now, can't I?"

"**May** you tell?" his mother said. "May you have permission to tell. Not are you able to tell."

"May I?" Dale asked.

"Yes. I guess so," his father said. "I imagine you've had a hard time keeping from exploding with the news."

"Yes. In one way," Dale said. "But in another way I was scared to tell. For fear it wouldn't happen."

"This means a lot to you, doesn't it, son?" Mr. Martin said.

"Yes, sir. It did. And does."

"Say, look at the time," his father said. "I'll have to sell a lot of nails and paint to pay for twenty acres. Coming to the store with me?"

"Might as well," Dale said. He had more than one idea running around in his mind. If he went to the store there might be a chance to bring up the subject of a pony. But if it stopped raining someone would be playing ball behind the general store and he could tell his news. "The day's just begun. Maybe there'll be time to do both," he decided.

He listened as his father told the real estate agent that the loan had been approved. He heard them plan to go to

33

Winchester together and close the deal. He saw his dad put the key to the farmhouse in his pocket.

As they hurried through the rain, Dale asked, "Is twenty acres a big farm, Dad?"

"No. A person couldn't make a living on that much land these days. The machinery it takes to put out a crop and harvest it would eat up many times as much money as the land could produce."

"Then how can we --"

"How can we afford it?" his father asked. "We have the store to earn our living. We'll rent out the one big field to some farmer. We're buying a home, not going into a moneymaking proposition."

"Will the farmer pay us money?"

"No, not cash," his father said. "We'll get a share of what he raises on our land, hay or corn, soybeans or oats, and maybe a little wheat."

"And we'll sell that stuff?" Dale asked.

"Some of it. Some we'll keep. To feed livestock. Pigs or calves -- or --"

"A pony?"

"Yes, a pony. We'll get to that. Don't you worry! And try not to be too impatient."

"I'll try," Dale said.

4

Dale was in a hurry for Sunday to come but he had other things to do before then. The sun came out that Saturday afternoon. More than a dozen boys were on the basketball court by the time he finished lunch. Three balls were being bounced on the rough concrete floor or shot through the air. Once in a while one fell through the rusty iron hoop.

No one seemed to notice Dale for a while, for maybe as long as five minutes. He stood on the grass at the end of the outdoor court and tried to catch Corky Painter's eye. "He's the first one I want to tell about the farm," Dale thought.

Dale was about ready to walk out and take part in the game when a ball came flying toward him. He barely got his hands out of his pockets in time to keep it from smashing into his face.

"Hey, guy!" Corky said. "You asleep or something?"

"No," Dale said. "Just not looking."

"Come on! Shoot a few," Corky said.

"Well, I will. But I wanted to tell you something first. We're going to move to a farm."

Corky didn't say anything. Dale couldn't figure out why. "I expected him to be excited. Like I am," Dale thought.

"Didn't you hear what --"

"I heard," Corky said. "I was just wondering. Will you have to change schools?"

"I don't know," Dale said. "No one said. And I never thought to ask."

For a minute a shadow seemed to creep over his happiness. He didn't like that. He didn't want this good thing spoiled.

"Where are you moving?" Corky asked.

37

"Out south. Out past Crystal Pool Bridge."

"Then you'll still come in to Parker City School. By bus. Don't you remember? A lot of kids in our class live out that way. Well, maybe not a lot. But the Craig boys do and Lois Canaday."

Dale was relieved. Not about living near Angie, but he was glad he wouldn't have to change schools.

Corky seemed to feel better too. "Come on over to my house," he said, "where we can hear better."

The Painters lived at the end of Fulton Street. Their side yard ran all the way to a farmer's field on the south edge of the town.

The boys sat down on a stone bench. The spring sunshine made it warm. Dale heard a buzzing sound. He looked all around but didn't see anything flying between him and the sky.

"They're bees," Corky said. "In the hollow tree along the fence. See them swarming around the hole?"

"Will they sting us?" Dale asked.

"Not if we don't bother them," Corky said. "And I wouldn't. This is the first day they've been out. At least I think so."

"It's been warm before."

"I know," Corky said. "But nothing was in bloom then. Nothing for them to use in making honey."

"Oh!" Dale said. "How'd you know so much about bees?"

"My Uncle Steve told me," Corky said. "He has a bunch of beehives on his farm. Out on Windsor Pike."

Dale wondered if they could have bees at their new place and maybe sell honey. "Do you have to know a lot to take care of them?"

"It helps," Corky said. "When you going to move?"

"I don't know for sure," Dale replied. "Soon I think. And hope."

"That's really great. For you I mean."

"Would you like to live in the country?" Dale asked.

"I don't think so," Corky said. "I like

39

to visit my uncle and granddad. But Parker City's okay with me."

For some reason Dale felt better. He wouldn't want Corky to be jealous. A lot of kids might be, and he wouldn't care as much what they thought. But Corky was special.

"We're going out to the farm tomorrow," Dale said. "Want to ask your mom if you can go along?"

"Maybe you better ask yours first," Corky said.

"Okay, I will. See you later."

"Don't you want to go back and play basketball? Wasn't that what you came for?"

"No, not really. Mainly to tell you about moving."

Dale walked home not quite knowing what he was going to do the rest of the day. His mother made up his mind for him as soon as he walked in the kitchen door.

First she handed him a warm oatmeal cookie. He could smell the cinnamon and see the bumps made by nuts and raisins.

40

"I'm glad you came home," she said. "I need some things from the grocery. For the picnic."

Dale almost said, "Where's Katie?" But that would've sounded as if he didn't want to go to the store. That wasn't in his mind at all. He just wondered where his sister was. He had thought as he came through the back gate, "Maybe Kate and I could begin packing stuff. Like our old toys and books." He couldn't quit thinking about moving.

"Your sister was supposed to go," Frances Martin said. "But Miss Colvin had to postpone her piano lesson for half an hour. And I need to get the chicken for tomorrow on to cook."

"Chicken?" Dale said. "I thought we were going to --"

"To picnic at the farm? We are. I'm making pressed chicken sandwiches."

"Yum!" Dale said. "I'll hurry for that! Any old time."

He started toward the door and then remembered about Corky. "Hey Mom! Is

it all right if Corky goes with us tomorrow?"

"Well, I don't see why not. Of course
he should ask his mother first."

"That's what **he** said," Dale replied.
"That I should ask **you** first. It sure takes
a lot longer to plan stuff when we have
to do all this asking."

"Perhaps," his mother said. "But it also
saves a lot of mix-ups."

"Is it okay if I go see Corky before --"
Dale started to ask. "No, I'd better do
that afterward. So the chicken can cook."

As he walked up Fulton and turned onto
Howard Street Dale tried to picture how
Parker City would be when he wasn't
here. Probably the same. The buildings
and people and everything. "The same
things will go on. I just won't be here,"
Dale thought. "Will anyone miss me --
besides Corky? Of course I'll see them at
school and we'll have to come to town a
lot. Dad's store is still here. And church."

As he headed home he tried to picture
the farm. He'd never seen it in the eve-

"My mom says it's okay with her if it is with your mother," Dale said.

ning. Could you see more of the sunset and hear a lot of sounds? Of birds or frogs or insects like katydids?

"Maybe I'll know how it sounds out there in the evening by this time tomorrow," he thought.

As he turned the corner he saw Corky coming toward him on his silver and blue Stingray bike. "I was going to hunt you up," Dale said. "My mom says it's okay with her if it is with yours."

"Mine said the same thing. She called your mom to find out what time I should come over. I'll be there by twelve-thirty. That's when you're leaving. See you!"

"See you!"

5

Corky was sitting at the end of the front walk when the Martins came home from church the next day. Dale saw him as soon as he rounded the corner and trotted ahead of his parents.

"I looked for you at church," Dale said. "Wondered if you were sick or something."

"No," Corky said. "No one called me to get up before they left. Just wrote a note."

"Left?"

"Yeah. For the races," Corky said with a trace of sadness in his voice.

Dale knew that Corky's dad was a race

car driver. He never heard of him win-
ning, only maybe a lap once in a while.
But every Sunday except in real cold
weather the Painters left for someplace
around the state. Sometimes they were
even gone from Friday night until late on
Sunday.

"You didn't want to go?" Dale said.

"No," Corky said scooting over to make
room for Dale on the sun-warmed cement.
"I don't like it much."

"Didn't you ever?"

"Not really. Too much noise and dirt
and danger. That's how I feel now anyway."

Dale looked at the sky. It was misty, as
if silver was mixed with blue. He didn't
see a cloud anywhere, not even a white
one.

"It sure is nice out," Corky said. "I
was scared it would rain."

"Why?" Dale asked. "We'd probably go
to the farm even if it did. And picnic in
the house."

"I didn't think of that," Corky said. "I

just figured I'd be stuck at home all day. By myself."

Dale glanced sideways at his friend. He looked sort of sad, "Is he left at home a lot? Is that why he wasn't too excited when I told him we were moving?"

All kinds of thoughts bumped into each other in Dale's mind. Some were grateful. He was glad his parents didn't go off doing what they wanted every weekend. They wouldn't leave him alone all day.

He also wondered what Corky would do when he was older -- and lonelier. Get to running around with the Craycraft twins maybe? That was a scary thought. The twins were accused of doing a lot of bad things. Some they did. Dale knew. They'd tried to get him to help them smear black paint on Miss Sanford's door after she held them back in the fourth grade.

Even if she was sort of grouchy sometimes, it was wrong to do bad things to her -- or anyone. But the twins didn't seem to know the difference between good and bad. Or if they did it didn't seem to change the way they acted.

"I'd better change my clothes," Dale said. "I couldn't have much fun if I had to be careful all the time. Want to come with me?"

"No. I'll wait here," Corky said. "That way you'll get ready sooner."

By the time Dale had changed into clean jeans and a T-shirt his mother had the lunch packed in the two-handled picnic basket.

"We'll eat as soon as we get there," she said as she climbed into the car. "For two reasons."

"I know one," Katie said. "It's time to eat. I'm hungry."

"True."

"But what's the other?" Dale's sister asked.

"Well," her mother said. "Once you all get scattered, I'd have a hard time rounding you up. Without yelling anyway. And I hope little Janie's asleep before too long."

48

"You really plan ahead, don't you?" Dale's father said.

"Someone has to," Frances Martin answered. "To keep things running smoothly -- or as much so as possible."

The children wanted to eat under the trees. Mrs. Martin thought it would be better to put the food on the folding table in the kitchen. "That way we can leave it up all day -- out of reach of the insect world."

So they compromised. Plates and cups were filled and carried to whichever place the picnickers chose. Katie took hers to the dormer upstairs, to the spot she was already calling her "Window on the World." Corky and Dale ate under the trees in the backyard. Mr. and Mrs. Martin unfolded canvas chairs on the front porch and the baby sat in a pillow-stuffed cardboard box.

"It sure is quiet out here," Corky said. "I can even hear myself chew."

"You always can," Dale said. "If you listen. But there are lots of other sounds too."

"Like what?"

"Like the crickets in the tall grass. And the frogs back along the creek."

"There's a river?" Corky asked.

"Not a river. Just a narrow little stream."

"Could we go? And swim?"

"It's not deep enough for swimming. But we could wade," Dale said.

Before sundown the boys had explored the creek for nearly a mile of its winding length. They waded in places where sand squished over their toes. They watched silvery minnows dart in and out of the gurgling ripples. Sometimes it was hard to tell what made the bright places in the water -- glints of sunshine, or shining scales of tiny fish.

They played in the barn, even in the dusty haymow after Dale's dad had checked to see if any floorboards were loose. The man who had farmed the place before hadn't moved all the hay. The boys tugged and shoved the bales to make a tunnel. They then piled loose hay over the top and crawled from one end to the other. Some of the hay fell in and made them cough and it scratched their arms, but they didn't care.

The light in the barn began to fade from shade to darkness. The boys climbed down the ladder and sat in the doorway of the feeding room.

"Do you reckon you'll have any animals?" Corky asked.

"Sure," Dale said. "Calves anyway. My dad's already said so."

"Pigs maybe?"

"No, not yet. The fences need fixing. Pigs could get under them and dig up the yard and the flower and vegetable garden my mom's going to plant."

Dale didn't bring up the subject of a pony. He thought about it, but he wasn't real sure when this dream would come true. "I'd better not say anything yet," he was thinking.

Corky chose that moment to ask, "Not any horses? They'd be the greatest."

"I know," Dale said. "Maybe later. Not

a horse exactly -- not a big one. Not a Shetland pony either. Something in between."

"That part I'd like," Corky said. "Not for racing or beating anyone. Just for fun."

Neither boy spoke for a minute or two. Birds twittered in the tree by the back gate. And a pigeon cooed softly from somewhere above them -- probably they roosted in the haymow.

"I reckon you'll be moving any day."

"Probably," Dale said.

Corky took a deep breath. Dale wanted to say, "You can come out any time."

"But he already knows that," Dale decided.

Katie ran out the back door and said, "Hey, you guys. I've called you three times. Mom says come eat so she can pack things."

The sun had disappeared behind the trees in the west by the time the Martins and Corky headed back toward Parker City. The moon didn't give much light. It

52

was only a sliver of pale gold in the dark blue sky.

Corky didn't say anything until Dale's father turned onto his street. "They're home. The porch light's on. And the upstairs one too. Thanks, everyone," he said as he climbed out of the car. "I had a great day!"

Dale thought of the house on the farm. It was dark now and probably looked lonely. But before long lights would shine in the windows at night.

6

The Martin family moved on Wednesday instead of waiting until the weekend. Dale's father closed the store at noon to help with the moving. By evening they were eating the first meal in their new home.

Dale and Katie wanted to skip school that day but their parents said no to this idea. "You'll ride out on bus Number 5," Mr. Martin said. "I've already told Dave Halliday -- he's the bus driver -- that he'll have two new passengers."

Dale usually walked home with Corky. This time he and his friend parted at the end of the walk. "What you going to do?" Dale asked before he boarded the bus.

"I have to go to my Grandma's again," Corky said. "No one's at home."

"Don't you like to go?"

"Not to this one. My other one's more fun. The one that lives here feels bad a lot. I can't do anything that makes noise."

"Well, I'll see you in the morning," Dale said.

"Yeah."

Dale's feelings went two ways. After he took a seat he looked out the window and he watched Corky cross the street. Corky sort of scuffed his feet like he didn't care much about getting where he was going. "And me! I can't wait to get to the farm," Dale thought.

After supper Dale unpacked his books and games and put things in or on the same pieces of furniture where they'd been before. "The house is different but home's the same," he thought as he put his mailbox bank on the top shelf in his desk bookcase. The bank was heavier than he

55

remembered. He untaped the little key from the bottom, unlocked the back panel, and dumped the coins on the bed.

"Might as well do this right while I'm at it," he thought. He took coin wrappers from between the pages of his savings account book. After he'd sorted the dimes, pennies, and nickles he added his figures. Five dollars and 89 cents not counting the quarters. He only had three of them, not enough to make a roll. "If I add what's here to what's in the bank in town, will I have enough for a pony maybe? Or enough to pay some, maybe half?" He opened his savings account book and reached for a pencil and paper.

His father came to the door as Dale was adding nine and eight. "What you got on your mind?"

Dale waited until he carried the one and added the last column of figures coming out with a total of $27.24. Then he grinned and said, "You know."

"Give me three guesses and I'll not need numbers two and three," his father said.

"You've got a pony on your mind."

"Yes, sir. But I know it's taken a lot of money for the place."

"Yes. It has. But something's come along."

"Like what?"

Dale's father sat down at the head of the bed and leaned his head back against the wall. "This has been a long day," he said. "It's surprising how much a family accumulates."

"But you didn't say. What came along?"

"Oh. Well I was out nailing our mailbox to the post when a man came down the road in a pony cart -- with a pony hitched to it, naturally. Didn't you see him?"

"I wasn't here. The mailbox was already up when we got off the bus."

"That's right. To make a long story short -- so we can all get to bed -- I got to talking to this man, Mr. Lennox. Real interesting fellow. Had a lot of tales to tell."

Dale wanted to say, "Hurry up." Grown-ups often used a lot of words when they weren't needed. He didn't want to hear any of the man's tales, at least not now.

"Anyway," Mr. Martin said. "He has ponies to sell. Three of them, as a matter of fact. I told him we'd get down there tomorrow evening."

"Down there?"

"Yes. Mr. Lennox is our nearest neighbor to the south. His land joins ours."

After his father left the room Dale got ready for bed but he didn't go to sleep right away. There weren't any curtains for his room yet, not even a window blind.

He could see a lot of the night sky. He knew the moon was out, even if he didn't catch a glimpse of it, because there was so much light. He tried to picture the ponies on the next farm but his father hadn't said what color they were. He wished he'd have remembered to ask. "But anyway I'm a lot closer to one than I've ever been in my whole life," Dale thought. "And we'll go down there tomorrow, and they're there right now."

The sun woke Dale the next morning.

There was nothing at the window to keep it out of his eyes. He didn't know if it was early or late. No one had called him.

He walked to the door and listened. There were no sounds from anywhere in the house. Then Dale thought of what his father had said the night before. "If there are ponies on the next farm maybe I could see them," Dale thought. "They might be in the next field."

He tiptoed downstairs and across the kitchen floor. He wasn't running away or doing anything bad. But his mother might worry, not want him to walk in wet grass or something. She worried a lot about such things.

His sneakers were wet by the time he'd crossed the barnyard. But he kept on, climbed the wire fence, and walked across the field where corn was growing, following a path between the rows. A toad with bumpy skin jumped ahead of him and went sideways into the next row. A big bird, maybe a hawk, seemed to float in the sky dipping its wings first one way then the other. "It's like the pilot who did stunts at the county fair," Dale thought.

Most of the time Dale kept his eyes on the pasture field beyond the next fence. He didn't see any movement and was thinking the ponies might be in a barn or someplace else on the farm. Then he heard a sound -- the pounding of running feet.

Dale ran toward the fence. Before he reached the edge of the field four ponies came in sight from behind a little hill. Their heads were high, their manes bouncing on their necks.

Dale's heart beat in his throat as he put his arms on the top wire and watched. None of the ponies were quite the same color. One was the color of the inside of walnut hulls and the other two were lighter.

"Dad said the man only has three for sale. Which one does he want to keep? I hope it's not the one with the cream-colored mane and tail," Dale thought. Already he'd made his choice. "I'd take an-

Dale was thinking the ponies might be in a barn or someplace else on the farm. Then he heard the pounding of running feet.

other one. But that is the one I really want for my own."

As Dale ran back across the field his wet shoes squished and his feet were a little cold but he didn't care. In his mind he saw a caramel-tan pony coming over a hill. And its ivory colored-mane was flapping and flying as it ran.

7

By eight o'clock that evening the tan pony with the honey-colored mane was in the boxed-in stall in the Martin barn. Things happened so fast that Dale could not believe his dream was really coming true. He'd expected to have to wait two or three days while his Dad and Mr. Lennox talked about the price and other things.

But his main fear was that his mother would try at the last minute to keep him from having a pony. He knew she wasn't in favor of the idea. She said things like, "I'm the one who's here most of the time. And I can't keep my eye on what's going on every minute."

Dale didn't understand what she meant. Why did he need to be watched all the time? "What does Mom think is going to happen?" he wondered.

There was a time during supper when it seemed that his mother might still try to stop them from bringing the pony home. Dale and his father had gone to the farm at half past five. Thirty minutes later Mr. Martin put his hand on Dale's shoulder. "Are you sure about this bay? Don't you want to look around?"

"No sir," Dale said. "I don't want to look anymore. Or wait any longer."

"Then we'll be back in an hour or less," Mr. Martin said. "Our supper's probably getting dried up."

Dale was hungry but he didn't want to take time to eat. He thought his father was unusually slow. It seemed like he buttered his rolls twice and ate his peas one at a time.

Dale's mother didn't say much. She

didn't even stay seated at the table. She kept jumping up to do things. She finally managed to eat a few bites. "Are you sure this animal is gentle? I mean you've only seen him this once."

"**Her**, Mom," Dale said.

"She's gentle," Dale's father said. "I'm sure."

"He sounds a little grouchy," Dale thought. "Like he's tired of Mom's worrying."

"What you going to call it?" She asked. "It can't keep on being it or she."

"Have you thought of a name, Katie?" Mr. Martin said.

"Not I. It's not mine. I don't like animals bigger than I am. They scare me."

"Is she like Mama?" Dale wondered.

"Dale, have you thought of a name?" his father asked.

"Yes. For a long time. I want it to be Cricket."

"Why that?"

"I don't know," Dale said. "It just seems right."

And so the light brown pony was named and found a new home on the same summer evening.

Dale led it home. He walked backward most of the time, so he could see the pony's prancing white feet and the flying mane. "She really steps pretty, doesn't she, Dad?" Dale asked. "Like she's proud."

"I think you're the one that's proud," Mr. Martin said. "It's a good thing there's very little traffic on this road. You haven't looked around more than twice since we headed home."

"Well, you're facing home," Dale said. "I don't think you'd let us get run over."

Dale's mother and sister came to the barn lot and looked at Cricket. Katie reached up and ran her fingers down the pony's face. "He's -- I mean, she's pretty."

"Want to sit on her back?" Mr. Martin asked.

"No -- I don't think so. Say, Dale, why aren't you riding?"

"I guess I never thought of it," Dale

said. "It was fun to lead her and watch. But I rode her at Mr. Lennox's place. Could I now, Dad?"

"Sure," Mr. Martin said. "It'll soon be dark so climb on -- remember how I showed you."

"I know."

Mrs. Martin and Katie went back to the house and Dale saw his father go to the barn. He was alone in the world with his pony. He felt a little scared. But he wouldn't want anyone to know that. "I'll get over it. When Cricket and I know each other better," he thought.

At first he held the bridle strap tightly, keeping the pony to a walk. They circled the barn lot three times before he eased his grip. Cricket responded and went into a slow trot. Dale felt that he was being rocked. The evening breeze bumped against his face and swished past his ears. His hair bounced on his forehead like Cricket's forelock flipped on her face.

Dale didn't want darkness to come. He wished the evening wouldn't end. He saw lights in the upstairs window and knew bedtime was near. His father came through the rectangle of light, out of the stable door. He gave a long whistle. Cricket turned and headed toward the light.

"How'd she know to do that?" Dale asked. "To come when you whistled?"

"It's not a question of how she knew," Mr. Martin said. "I'm the one who had to learn. I watched her come across the field when Mr. Lennox whistled -- while you were looking at the carts and saddles."

Dale slid down from Cricket's back. His legs felt a little numb. Then prickles stung his feet as he walked into the barn. He put fresh hay in the sloping manger while his father unbuckled the bridle and hung it on a wooden peg.

"Won't she be thirsty?" Dale asked.

"That's right. We should have led her to the tank. Here, I'll loop this rope around her neck and you lead her out while I spread this bale of straw for bedding."

Cricket followed Dale, her hooves clip-clopping on the gravel. Dale watched as the pony took long slurps of water. The sun was down and a gold sliver of moon had risen above the trees in the east. An owl's hoot came from the orchard.

The pony lifted her head and looked across the fields. She whinnied three times. "Does she hear the other ponies?" Dale wondered. "Is she homesick?" He put one arm across her neck and patted her face. "Don't you worry," he said. "We're going to take good care of you. You'll get used to us pretty soon."

"Everyone must have gone to bed," Mr. Martin said as they walked in the kitchen door. "No wonder! Look at the time. That school bus will be pulling up at the front gate before you're ready."

"I wish I could stay at home tomorrow," Dale said. "But I know I can't."

"No way," his father said. "Unless you play sick. Then your mama wouldn't let you ride Cricket."

"I know."

Dale had a little trouble getting to

sleep. When he shut his eyes he felt as if he was still on Cricket's back. When he opened them he tried to picture how Corky would look and what he'd say when he heard they'd bought a pony.

"Will he be glad for me?" Dale wondered. "Even if animals aren't very important to him, he could see how I feel. Maybe he will and maybe he won't."

8

It was hard for Dale to keep his mind on what he was supposed to be doing at school the next day. He was thinking of what he'd done the evening before or what he'd be doing when he got home.

He had to work three problems over and this was unusual. He understood fractions a lot better than he did other things, like decimals. During social studies the teacher said, "Where are you, Dale? I've asked you the same question twice."

"I didn't even hear him the first time," Dale thought. "I'd better begin paying attention or my grades may go down."

He had a disappointed feeling about something. Was it always this way? Did great feelings and bad ones have to be mixed? Like changed feelings about Corky were spoiling the fun of having Cricket -- just a little.

He'd known that Corky wouldn't be excited about the news that the Martins had bought a pony. "I did think he'd listen and maybe ask questions," Dale thought. "But he didn't even stop. Just ran past me. Chasing after Todd Craycraft. I guess he's with him a lot now."

The classroom seemed dark when Dale walked in from a gym class. He walked to the window before going to his seat. Smoky clouds tumbled across the sky. "I reckon it's going to rain. So I can't ride Cricket tonight," Dale thought.

A shower did come but it only lasted a few minutes. The raindrops which pelted against the windows evaporated within ten minutes. And the sun was shining when Dale boarded the bus. He took an outside seat and watched kids come out the doors

72

in two lines and branch off in different directions. He didn't see Corky.

"Saving this seat?" someone asked.

Dale turned, saw Ronnie Craig, and shook his head. "No. Unless it's for you."

"I didn't see you last night. I was absent. Dean told me you were on. You move or something?"

"Yes. We bought a farm -- between here and a place called Windsor. Wherever that is."

"It's where I live," Ronnie said. "Did you want to move?"

"Sure," Dale said.

"I wouldn't," Ronnie said. "But some kids don't seem to care one way or the other. Maybe because they don't ever stay home much."

"Do you -- I mean won't your folks let you run around?"

"Some," Ronnie said. "But we have rules. My mom says our backyard is as good as the neighbor's."

The bus had pulled onto the highway and Dale could feel the vibrations of the motor under his feet. He couldn't hear it because of the talking and yelling. He hadn't thought of school buses being so noisy.

"We had rules too, back in Parker City. I sort of like them. You can depend on something." Dale looked out the window after the bus left the highway for the gravel road. "I live out here three or four miles."

"Well, Windsor's on down at the end of this road. Maybe you could come see me. Do you have a bike?"

"Yes," Dale said. He wanted to tell Ronnie he could ride his pony. But he might not think that was so great.

They didn't say anything for two or three minutes. Then Ronnie leaned over and pointed. "Did you see that! Look across the field." A silver gray riding horse was running along a fence. "Man, that's one fine horse!"

"You like animals?"

"I sure do. 'Specially horses. But we don't have room for one. And no barn."

74

"We do," Dale said. "And I have a pony. Just got her last night."

"Oh, man!" Ronnie said. "You're lucky!"

"I know. Do you think you could come back to see me? Is it too far to walk?"

"I don't know," Ronnie said. "Not until I see where you live."

When the bus slowed to let Dale and Katie off Ronnie said, "This isn't far from Windsor. I can ride my bike easy. If Mom lets me. Do you have to ask your mother if someone can come?"

"Yes," Dale said. "I do. And they don't even know each other."

"Yes, but that isn't a bother to moms. They talk anyway. We're in the phone book. See you maybe."

"What was that boy talking about?" Katie asked as they walked up the lane.

"About coming down, maybe. He has to ask his mother."

"I guess some things are the same in the country as in town," Katie said.

"It's some mothers who are the same as others," Dale said.

They went around to the back door. Their mother met them. "The baby's asleep," she said. "So walk easy. She's been restless all day. Knows she's in a strange place, I guess."

"I'm starved," Katie said.

"That's nothing new," her mother replied. "I baked some gingerbread. You can have some -- with milk. How about you, Dale?"

"Well, I'm hungry -- but I want to see about Cricket first."

His mother started to say something, then stopped and ran one knuckle back and forth across her forehead. "I meant to tell you. Your little sister's not the only one who's been homesick. I've heard nickering sounds from the stable."

Dale went upstairs to change his clothes, skipping every other step. "Mama wanted to say something else," Dale thought. "She always acts the same when we talk about a pony. Like she doesn't say what she's really thinking. What could it be?"

Cricket turned her head when Dale

76

Dale swung onto the pony's back and rode around the barn lot.

walked into the stall. Then she arched her neck and made nodding motions." She acts glad to see me. Like maybe she knows me already."

He had to stretch to fasten the buckle on the leather bridle. "That's because she's part Arabian, not all Shetland. It's a good thing, too. I'd soon be too big for a regular pony."

Cricket took a long drink after Dale led her to the watering tank. Then she raised her head and looked across the fields. "I'd like to take her over there to see the other horses. But I don't know what would happen. Could one jump the fence? Could I get Cricket to come back with me?"

He swung onto the pony's back and rode around the barn lot several times. He learned to lean to keep from sliding off when Cricket turned. "It'd be better with a saddle," he thought. "But I'd better not say anything about that. I'm lucky as it is."

Ronnie came down the road within a few minutes, pedaling so hard that Dale was afraid he'd not be able to turn in the driveway.

"I guess our mothers talked," Dale said as Ronnie leaned his bike against the yard fence.

"They still are," Ronnie said. "Or they were when I left. Like they'd known each other forever. Your mom's supposed to tell me when it's five o'clock."

The tan pony with the cream-colored mane made many trips around the grassy barnyard. Ronnie said they should take turns but Dale told him, "You go on. I'm here more."

Dale picked up a handful of pebbles from the lane. He sat down and leaned against the front of the barn and threw the stones one at a time at an imaginary target. But his eyes were on Cricket most of the time. This was the first time that he'd watched her feet move. "She walks in a kind of rhythm;" he thought. "Her feet keep time. Like music. Like Miss Colvin's -- the thing that keeps time -- the metronome."

9

The days before school was out moved as slowly as the mud turtles which waddled along the creek. The days were longer but Dale didn't have much more time to ride his pony.

There was work to be done on the farm. Springtime was for planting. Mr. Lennox came down the road on his tractor to plow the garden, Mrs. Martin's flower beds, and two small fields. Dale climbed up on the wooden fence post on one side of the gate and watched the tractor chug up and down the strip of land where his mother would grow her cannas. The points of the three shining blades, which Mr. Lennox called plowshares, dug into the grass and rolled back a long hump of black soil.

Dale didn't know his father was home until Mr. Martin walked up to the fence. "Can you plant things now, Dad? In all those bumps?"

"No, no," Mr. Martin said. "They'll work it down with a cultipacker or disk or harrow. They're farm tools."

"There sure is a lot to learn about farming!"

"About everything," his father said. "The more discoveries some people make the more the rest of us have to learn."

"That's kind of scary," Dale said. "Seems like I have all I can do to keep up now."

The Martins rarely ate their evening meal before nine o'clock now except on rainy evenings when they couldn't work outside. The baby went to sleep long before the rest of the family sat down at the kitchen table. Someone, usually Katie, had to stay in the house with her. Dale didn't think it was fair that his sister got to watch television more than he could. But he didn't complain much because he knew that he rode Cricket whenever he had a few minutes. "And I'd ride more if I wasn't working," he thought.

Sometimes Ronnie came down and helped if Dale had to work. The boys' mothers had found time to get acquainted and all members of both families exchanged visits. One evening the week after school was out, Katie said, "We almost never go to Parker City anymore."

"I go every day -- except Sunday," her father said. "And we all go to church there then."

"But we don't visit anyone."

"Who would you like to see?" her mother asked.

"Oh, I don't know of anyone in particular," Katie said. "But it seems sort of funny. Like we don't live anywhere. Just in between places."

"Well, maybe you could ask someone out to stay all night with you."

"From where? Parker City or Windsor?"

"That's for you to decide," her mother said.

"I guess I could have someone from either town," Katie said. "Girls from both places are in my class."

"One at a time, please," her mother said. "When there are three, one's left out."

Dale's feelings about living on a farm changed during the summer. One day in the middle of July he realized how different country life was from what he'd expected. His mother and sisters went into Muncie to shop and have the baby's picture taken.

"Couldn't I stay here?" Dale asked.

"No, indeed. You should know better than to ask. You'd be out on that pony. What would happen if you fell? Besides, it's looking a little stormy outside. You can never tell where lightning will strike."

"But I won't have any fun in town. And it's too hot to get dressed up."

"Well, I guess you could stay with your

father. Or visit friends. I can drop you off.
Then you can come home at suppertime."

"Why do we eat supper at night now?"
Katie asked. "It used to be dinner."

"Because," her mother said, "most people out here say supper."

Dale hadn't been in the hardware store enough to know what was new. He walked around stopping to read price tags on electric lanterns, barbecue grills, and chain saws. When he saw the sun come through the clouds, he went outside and sat on the concrete step. "Things are sure quiet around here," he thought. "Where is everybody?"

He guessed that some people he knew were at the swimming pool out at Maxville. Others could be playing basketball. But it was pretty hot for that. Then he remembered what his Dad had said that morning. "I had a run on baseball caps this week. It's little league play-offs. Girls have started a fad. They wear the caps backward. Some paint initials all over them with felt-tip pens."

Dale hadn't thought much about missing playing on a little league team. This was partly because he had a choice. His parents said they'd see that he got into practices and games. But living in the country was new, Ronnie didn't play baseball, and there wasn't enough time to ride Cricket as it was."

"It's strange," Dale thought as he rested one elbow on a knee and his chin in a cupped hand. "Out there I didn't feel left out. In here where stuff is going on I do."

"Hi ya, Dale," someone called from across the street.

Dale looked up to see Tom Craycraft coming toward him. "What you doing?" Tom asked. "Helping your Dad?"

"No. I just came in while my mother went in town. Where's everybody?"

"Mostly at the ball park."

"Why aren't you?"

"I don't play," Tom said. "I got kicked off."

"How about Todd and Corky?"

"Oh, they're still on the team. But

mostly they warm the bench. That coach has his pets."

Dale didn't say anything. The Craycraft twins were always mad at someone and almost always put teachers down.

"It must be neat," Tom said as he sat down on the other end of the step. "Out there with trees and a creek and even your own horse."

"It's fine," Dale said. "But it's not like you make it seem. Not like a park. I mean we work -- hard and late sometimes."

"You don't like it, huh?"

"Sure I like it," Dale said. "It's just that most people don't see both sides of living on a farm. I guess I didn't until now."

"I wouldn't go for that. The work part would be a drag."

"It's not that bad," Dale said. "Besides, I don't have to worry about what to do next. There's always something."

"I'd better move on," Tom said. "See you around."

As Tom went down the alley Dale thought, "Is that why guys like Tom and Todd get in so much trouble? Is it because they don't have anything else much to do?"

Dale went up to the drugstore for a strawberry soda. He didn't see anyone he knew except some girls. He didn't stay any longer than it took to sip the last pink bubbles. He was glad to get back to the hardware store and was relieved that Uncle Deke was going to take over until closing time.

"The sky's clear now," Dale's father said. "And we'll have time to clean out the calf stall and put in fresh straw."

"You going to borrow Mr. Lennox's tractor?"

"Not borrow -- rent. I'm hoping we can buy one at a farm sale by this time next year. The calves we have will be ready to sell by then."

Dale didn't like to be around the black Angus calves. His father had warned him, "They're wild. You can't make pets of them. Don't ever get in the same stall or field with one, unless I'm near."

"Are all cows like the Angus?" Dale asked as they headed toward home.

"What do you mean? You know there are several types."

"I mean wild?" Dale said. "I don't like being around animals I'm afraid to touch or be near."

"Well, maybe I was a little hasty when I bought these calves. I still have a lot to learn. Next time I'll look around for Herefords or Shorthorns. But in a way it's a good thing you don't like the Angus."

"Why?"

"Because if you were attached to them and made pets of them, you wouldn't want to see them sold."

10

It was August before anyone in the Martin family began to talk about going on a vacation. They'd been busy planting, pulling weeds, and painting fences, rooms, and buildings.

By this time Mrs. Martin's cannas were beginning to bloom. She hadn't been able to buy as many of the knobby bulbs as she wanted. Dale thought she had too many when he helped place the roots in the long rows.

"Next year there'll be more," Mrs. Martin said. "I'll be able to divide these. In time I'll have some to sell."

Dale didn't think canna blossoms were as pretty as lots of other flowers. But if his mother liked them that was all right with him.

"What you planning to do when you get rich from selling bulbs?" Mr. Martin asked one summer evening.

They were sitting on the front porch waiting for the house to cool enough for sleeping. Dale lay on the porch floor with his head resting on one arm. He could see the moon through the posts of the porch railing. "It's like a golden ball with black up-and-down stripes," he thought.

The porch swing squeaked as it moved forward, then back. Dale was getting a little sleepy.

"Any ideas about where to go on vacation?"

"No," Dale's mother said. "I hadn't even thought about going anyplace."

"I know where I'd like to go," Katie said. "Back to the woods."

Dale sat up and tried to see his sister's face. Was she kidding?

"What made you think of that?" Mrs. Martin asked.

"I've been thinking about it ever since we moved out here. There's that woods and real neat creek. But we never have time to wade or explore -- almost never anyway."

"You know something," Dale said. "She's right. That's a great idea -- especially for a girl."

"We could camp out, I suppose," Mr. Martin said, "and still be close enough to look out for the livestock."

"And we could take Cricket back -- tie her some place. Can we do it, Dad?"

"We'll think about it. Now it's time to rest up for tomorrow."

Plans for the at-home camping were made by the end of the next week. "One thing I want all of you to understand is that I'm not going to cook the whole time," Dale's mother said. "We'll have a lot of sandwiches and quick-heat foods."

"That's good. You'll have your fill of them in those four days."

"Is that all the longer we are going to stay?" Dale asked.

"Yes it is," his mother said. "Your father doesn't feel he can afford to be away from the store any longer. And I'll probably have my fill of loafing by then -- and of sleeping on cots."

Mr. Martin borrowed one tent and brought two small ones from the store for Dale and Katie. They decided to take enough food back for a day at a time. We can get what we need when we go up to feed the livestock."

Mrs. Martin invited her sisters and Mr. Martin's brother's family to come back to the woods when they could get away. And the Craig family came for supper on Tuesday evening.

Dale and his father followed the creek all the way to White River and explored the Indian mounds two or three times. Mrs. Martin read four books and knitted a pink sweater for the baby between naps and walks in the woods.

The weather made the four days pleasant. No thunderstorms came to drive them to the house. The temperature went up to 99 degrees on Wednesday but there was shade to sit in and cool creek water for wading.

The Craig family came at half past four. Dale saw Ronnie and his brother, Dean, racing ahead of their parents who were carrying a basket and gallon thermos jug.

"We meant to feed you," Dale's mother said as Mrs. Craig came through the wide gate.

"I know, but our sweet corn is ready to eat -- lots of it -- and Joe brought home a half bushel of muskmelons. We just brought our surplus."

"Should we go feed the calves before we eat?" Dale asked.

"Why don't you do that," his mother said. "There's time."

The boys caught up with Cricket who'd had a free run of the woods for three days. They took turns riding her to the house. They hadn't dared to try to find out if she'd carry two on her back at the same time.

As they came within sight of the barn Dale saw that something was wrong. A black Angus steer was nibbling grass in the barn lot and another was starting through the feedlot gate.

"What'll I do? They could get out on the road. There's no time to call Dad," he thought.

"You run back to the woods, Ron," Dale shouted, "I'll stay on Cricket and try to head them off."

Dale felt his heart thumping in his chest as he guided his pony around the straying calves. His dad had warned him about getting close to the excitable cattle. "Surely they won't charge at Cricket," Dale thought. "I hope she can outrun them."

Dale looked up and down the road when he got to the end of the driveway. No cars were in sight. That was good.

All kinds of thoughts bumped into each other in his mind. Should he sit and wait until help came? Would the one calf go

94

back into the pen if he edged Cricket toward it? What was the best thing to do? The safest?

The pony made the first move on her own. She tossed her head up and took a few prancing steps in the direction of the calf. "You're not afraid of any old Angus, are you?" Dale said as he leaned forward and patted Cricket's neck.

The calf stood for a minute, then turned and started toward the others, swinging its stubby tail to flick away biting flies. As it neared the gate the other stray wheeled around and walked alongside.

"Man, that was easy," Dale thought. "For once they acted tame." He glanced down the lane toward the woods and saw his father, Mr. Craig, and Dean coming toward the barn. He was ready to slide off Cricket's back when three or more gray and white pigeons flew from the square door in the haymow. Things happened so quickly that Dale didn't have time to count birds.

He heard the cooing calls and the whir

of flapping wings. So did the Angus calves. They raised their heads from the hayrack in the middle of the feedlot, still chewing, with wisps of dry grass wiggling at the corners of their wide mouths.

"They might begin to run any minute and stampede," Dale thought. "Do I dare get off and shut that gate? Or should I wait until Dad gets here?"

11

Dale decided to wait at the gate and stay on Cricket's back until help came. He glanced around looking for something to throw in case one of the calves acted like it was going to run. He saw a stick, a sharply pointed board from the old gate. It wasn't very thick but was long and pointed at one end.

"I'll have time to step off and get it." He had the piece of board in his hand and was throwing a leg over Cricket's back when the pigeons circled back. Any other time he would have loved watching their wide wings flutter and listening to their soft trilling calls. Now he wished they'd go away or at least be quiet.

The return of the birds was like a trigger to the Angus nearest the gate. It shot toward Dale. He didn't have time to think. He slid to the ground and ran to shut the gate. But Cricket moved faster. She tossed her head and lunged toward the steer. Dale was afraid there'd be a head-on collision. "Maybe I can head the calf off," Dale thought. He threw the pointed stick without taking time to aim. As it sailed through the air he wanted to run and bring it back. It was sailing straight toward Cricket's head!

In those seconds Dale felt the greatest pain he'd ever known. His mouth was dry and his eyes were wet as he watched Cricket rear up on her hind feet and throw her head backward. The pointed stick hit Cricket in her eye, quivered back and forth, then fell to the ground.

Dale put his arm across his face as he saw blood. He forgot all about danger to himself. He'd hurt his pony. He didn't

"Maybe I can head the calf off," Dale thought. He threw the pointed stick without taking time to aim.

even realize that his Dad had climbed the fence at the side of the feedlot, until he saw him take hold of the bridle.

The next two hours were a blur of ache and worry. Dean Craig ran back to the woods to tell the others what had happened. Mr. Craig called the veterinarian and Ronnie brought cold water and a sponge to hold to Cricket's face.

Dale just stood there with one hand on the pony's neck and the other rubbing her face. "I'm sorry," he whispered over and over. Once in a while he'd ask, "Is it bad, Dad? Will she be blind?"

"I'm not sure. That's why we called Doc Cates."

The veterinarian had trouble examining the wound. Cricket kept tossing her head and nickering. It was like she was crying. Finally Doc Cates turned to Dale. "You'd better come up here, boy. Maybe she'll hold still for you."

"I don't see why she would," Dale thought. "I'm the one who hurt her." But as he talked and patted, Cricket became quiet. Once in a while she pawed at the ground with one foot or made sad sounds but she didn't lunge or toss her head.

"Well, there's some damage," the veterinarian said. "But I think she'll keep the sight in that eye. It's lucky the stick caught the corner of the eye and not the center."

"Should we do anything?" Mr. Martin asked.

"No. I'll give her a shot to counter infection. I'd keep her away from other animals and out in the open. I think nature will take care of the rest. I'll stop by to check on her in a day or two."

Dale was relieved but not happy. He didn't know what he wanted to do, run to his room and be alone or stay near Cricket. Both maybe. Instead he went back to the woods with the others. The mothers and Katie asked what the doctor said and were glad that Cricket wouldn't be blind. Then they went on serving food, eating, and talking about other things.

"They act like nothing happened," Dale thought. "It's like I'm the only one that

101

cares. Is that because I'm the one who hurt Cricket?"

He didn't want to eat or even put food on his plate. But he knew that there'd be a lot of fuss if he didn't. He had to swallow hard to get half a hamburger and four pieces of melon down his throat. He also had to watch for the right time when no one was looking his way to toss the rest of the sandwich into the bushes.

He was glad about one thing. His dad had let him lead Cricket back to the woods. "But we'll have to tie her to the fence and take her to the stall for the night. It wouldn't do for her to wander loose. A branch or twig might scratch her eye."

Dale left the others twice and walked over to the fence. He didn't really want to look at the eye but he did anyway. It was swollen a little and looked a little milky. "But maybe the medicine does that," Dale thought.

Cricket rubbed his shoulder with her nose. She didn't act as if anything had changed. Dale climbed the fence and pulled several handfuls of red clover and she ate the grass just like always.

The Craigs stayed until long after the sun went down. But the moon was full and the night wasn't dark. The air was a misty gray. Any other time Dale would have enjoyed watching the flames of the campfire die to glowing coals. Any other time he would have enjoyed the stories Mr. Craig told about the Indians who lived in this part of Indiana and the oil drillers who came to find a fortune and had to move on to get rich in other states. For a little while Dale did forget about what he'd done to Cricket. This was when Mr. Craig recalled stories of when natural gas was discovered. "People went crazy. They stuck iron pipes in the ground and let gas burn day and night. Wasted fuel they have to pay for now."

Dale tried to picture how it had been with flames making the night as light as day. It was harder for him to see why the gas was left to burn in daylight. Wasn't there a way to shut off the flow?

Dale and his father walked to the house with their visitors. Cricket trailed along at the end of the bridle strap stopping sometimes to munch grass. She could still see clover, even in moonlight.

Ronnie hadn't said much to Dale since the accident. He'd stayed with him, sat close by the campfire, but hadn't talked much. As they walked up the lane Dale realized how quiet his friend had been. "Does he know how I feel?" Dale wondered. "That I don't want to talk?"

Somehow this thought made Dale feel better. So he forced himself to say, "We'll be camping out one more day. Why don't you ask if you can come down? All day, if you want?"

"I'd like to," Ronnie said. "I have one yard to mow in the morning. But I could get here by ten. If you're sure it's okay."

"I'm sure," Dale said. "Maybe we'll have time to find that place where the wild grapevine grows over the water. The place your dad said he used to play."

104

"If someone hasn't hacked it down," Ronnie said.

"Well, we can look. See you."

As he walked back to the woods Dale was a little surprised at himself. "How can I look forward to doing something tomorrow when today was so bad?" he wondered.

12

Dale's mother was sitting near the camp-fire in a folding metal chair. She'd put a few chunks of wood on the coals. Bright flames were curling and flickering in the night air around them. Once in a while sparks winked in the darkness.

"Are the girls asleep?" Mr. Martin asked.

"Yes. Janie must be getting used to camping. She curled up in her port-a-crib and was in dreamland before I spread the mosquito netting. I looked in on Katie -- and the book she just had to finish was on the ground."

"Well, I think I'll turn in too," Dale's father said. "It's been a long day."

"Don't either of you want anything to eat?" Fran Martin asked. "You didn't eat much, Dale. And that was hours ago."

"I guess I wasn't very hungry."

"How about now?"

"I guess I am a little. But I can't think of anything that sounds good. Unless it's a peanut-butter cookie."

"Help yourself," his mother said. "And there's milk in the ice chest."

Dale came back and pulled a canvas-seated chair up closer to the fire. The air was cooler and a soft breeze made the leaves of the trees whisper and rustle.

Night sounds came from all directions. "The country isn't really quiet," he thought. "You just hear its noises where there aren't cars and a lot of people." An owl's hooting and sad cry came from somewhere in the tall trees. When Dale stopped chewing he could hear the squeaky call of crickets. As he listened tears began to roll down his cheeks and he couldn't keep his shoulders from shaking. He hadn't cried when he'd hit his pony, just shed a few tears. Now he sobbed and he couldn't choke back the sounds, couldn't keep his mother from hearing.

She didn't move or say anything until the sobs died away into jerky hiccoughs. Then she came over and sat down at the side of his chair. She took Dale's hands in hers and began to talk. And her first words were, "I think I know exactly how you feel."

"How can she?" Dale thought. "She never had a pony. I don't think she even likes animals much."

"This is why I wasn't in favor of you having a pony. You wanted it so badly. And I knew that if anything happened -- well, I knew how you'd suffer. But the pain you felt today is the worst kind. Because you caused it."

Dale slid to the ground and leaned against his mother. A boy his age might be too big to cry and lean on someone's shoulder. But that's what he did.

108

His mother put one arm around him and rubbed the scar in the crook of his arm with the fingers of the other hand. "Every time I see this wound I feel a little of the pain you feel now. I caused this. I let you be hurt by my carelessness. I set a cup of hot coffee too close to the edge of the table. And my little boy reached for his ball and tipped the scalding drink on his arm."

"But, Mom, it's all right now. I don't even think about the puckered place. Besides, you didn't mean to hurt me."

"I know. And that's what you should realize now. You didn't intend to hit Cricket."

"No, I didn't. But she may not know that."

"Then how do you know I wouldn't hurt you purposely?"

"Because I know you love me," Dale said softly.

"Oh, Dale," his mother said. "Those words make me feel so good. All these years I've felt guilty. And that feeling made me want to protect you from having the same kind of pain."

Mrs. Martin got up and sat in the chair and Dale leaned against her legs. He was not ready to go to bed. Not yet. He didn't want this time of talking to end. "Maybe that's because I feel a lot better already," Dale thought.

"Don't you think Cricket knows how you feel about her?"

"I hope so. She acted the same, rubbed her face on my shoulder, and ate the clover I picked."

Dale thought of the pony up in the barn. He hoped her eye wasn't hurting and that she wouldn't bump it on anything in the dark. "Or did Dad leave the light on in the feeding room?" Dale wondered. "I know what I'm going to do first thing in the morning. I'll go up and see how she is and bring her back here."

He was getting sleepy. His eyelids began to droop and shut out the firelight. But one thought was still a little fuzzy in his mind.

"Mom," he said. "You make it sound like the hurt's not so bad when we love someone."

"Yes. I think love helps. Don't you?"

"I'm not sure," Dale said. "I'm kind of mixed up. In a way it's worse. I mean, I wouldn't have felt so terrible if I'd hit an Angus or someone else's pony. Bad, but not like this."

"That's true," his mother said. "Just like I wouldn't want to burn any child. But to do it to the son who's so dear to me --"

"I guess loving makes us hurt."

"Sometimes yes. But it also heals the pain. And that's something I didn't fully understand myself until tonight. You've helped me. Now do you think you can go to sleep?"

"Yes. But I'm sort of hungry. Is it all right if I take a couple more cookies to bed with me?"

"I guess so," his mother said. "It's you who will have to sleep on the crumbs. Good-night, Daley.

"Mom's not called me that for a long time," Dale thought. "Not since she understood that it was a baby name to me. But it's all right this time."

He crawled into the pup tent and managed to change into pajamas without crumbling the cookies. He propped himself up on his elbow while he ate one, but he couldn't finish the second. He thumped his pillow and doubled it to make it as thick as he could. Eating had made him wider awake. He thought ahead to the next day. Would they find the wild grapevine which made a swing over the water? Would it be so high they'd be afraid to jump into the river? How deep would the stream be?

Even after his eyelids shut out the sight of the pale gold moon in the deep blue sky, Dale saw pictures. In one, Cricket was running across a green field with her cream-colored mane flying in the wind. In another he was riding her at the county fair pony show and her prancing feet carried him to the judges' stand so a purple ribbon could be tied on her bridle.

The last pictures before he fell asleep were of the tan pony running to the fence when he whistled and nudging his shoulder with her nose.

Jerry Burney photo

Dorothy Hamilton was born in Delaware County, Indiana, where she still lives. She received her elementary and secondary education in the schools of Cowan and Muncie, Indiana. She attended Ball State University, Muncie, and has taken work by correspondence from Indiana University, Bloomington, Indiana. She has attended professional writing courses, first as a student and later as an instructor.

Mrs. Hamilton grew up in the Methodist Church and participated in numerous school, community, and church activities until the youngest of her seven children was married.

Then she felt led to become a private tutor.

This service has become a mission of love. Several hundred girls and boys have come to Mrs. Hamilton for gentle encouragement, for renewal of self-esteem, and to learn to work.

The experiences of motherhood and tutoring have inspired Mrs. Hamilton in much of her writing.

Seven of her short stories have appeared in quarterlies and one was nominated for the American Literary Anthology. Since 1967 she has had fifty serials published, more than four dozen short stories, and several articles in religious magazines. She has also written for radio and newspapers.

Mrs. Hamilton is author of **Anita's Choice, Christmas for Holly, Charco, The Killdeer, Tony Savala, Jim Musco, Settled Furrows, Kerry, The Blue Caboose, Mindy, The Quail, Jason, The Gift of a Home, The Eagle,** and **Neva's Patchwork Pillow.**